No Means No!

Teaching children about personal boundaries, respect and consent;
empowering kids by respecting their choices and their right to say, 'No!'

by Jayneen Sanders

illustrated by Cherie Zamazing

No Means No!
Educate2Empower Publishing an imprint of
UpLoad Publishing Pty Ltd
Victoria Australia
www.upload.com.au

First published in 2015

Written by Jayneen Sanders
Illustrations by Cherie Zamazing
Designed by Ben Galpin

Cataloguing-in-Publication Data

National Library of Australia

Creator: Sanders, Jayneen, author.

Title: No means no! : teaching children about personal boundaries,
                respect and consent; empowering kids by respecting their choices
                and their right to say, 'no!' / Jayneen Sanders ; Cherie Zamazing.

ISBN: 9781925089141 (hbk.)

Subjects: Respect for persons.
                Personal space.
                Autonomy in children.
                Interpersonal relations.

Other Authors/Contributors:
                Zamazing, Cherie, illustrator.

Dewey Number: 158.2

Dedication

To my three amazing and inspiring
daughters whose voices have always
been strong and crystal clear!
Proud of you all!
J.S.

♡♡♡

Note to the Reader

It is crucial that our children, from a very young age, are taught to have a clear, strong voice in regards to their rights — especially about their bodies. In this way, they will have the confidence to speak up when they are unhappy or feel uncomfortable in any situation. A strong, confident voice as a young child converts to a strong, confident pre-teen, teenager and adult. With the prevalence today of online and offline bullying and various forms of abuse, such as physical, emotional and sexual; our young people need to learn (from a young age) to always speak up when their rights are not being respected.

My aim in writing this book is to empower young children so they can grow up into empowered adults. When a child, teenager or adult says, 'No!' to any form of coercion, this should be immediately respected. A world where 'No!' does actually mean 'No!' can be a world with far less violence and increased respect for humankind. By educating our children to have true respect for one another, this world can be a much safer and more positive place.

Read this book with your child often. The Discussion Questions on pages 24 and 25 are important in helping you to draw out the learning for your child.

Some points to note:

→ In most cases, each character 'asks' the little girl's permission before or while engaging with her. This is important to note, as children (and teenagers and adults) should always be given the opportunity to consent or not. Just as importantly, they need to learn to ask when engaging with another person (especially as they grow into adulthood). If we force a child to show physical affection, what we are basically saying to them is that their wishes don't matter. The child should give hugs and kisses willingly, and all adults need to respect the child's choice. You may also wish to explain to people your child comes regularly into contact with, that 'manners' involve treating each other with respect and not forced and 'consent-assumed' physical contact.

→ It is important to note that adults outside the family also ask permission from children, e.g. when a child is at the dentist, the dentist should ask the child if it is okay to look inside his or her mouth. This models respect for another person's personal boundaries.

→ The scenarios in this book relate to personal space and a child's autonomy over their body. Of course, if a child is told that it's time to go to bed, or to clean their teeth, then, No Means No! is not an appropriate response. Another situation might be where a teacher or parent asks a child to hold hands with another person for safety reasons. Use the Discussion Questions on pages 24 and 25 to establish with your child when it is their right to say, 'No!' You could list these scenarios together, so the guidelines are clear for you and your child.

→ Lastly, as your child grows, provide them with choice, e.g. Would you like eggs or cereal for breakfast? What will you choose to wear today? This way your child has a say in decisions that relate directly to them. This children's book is about giving children choice, respecting their choices and personal boundaries, asking them for their consent and empowering them as they grow into adulthood .

When Auntie Jeanie asks me for a kiss,
and I don't want to ...

No Means No!

I can choose to blow her a kiss,
shake her hand, or give her a high five,
but if I don't want a hug or a kiss ...

No Means No!

When it's bath time and my mother asks if she can wash and dry my private parts, and I say, 'No thanks, I can do it all by myself' …

No Means No!

I can wash and dry my own private parts today,
tomorrow or the next day because my body
is my body and I am the BOSS of it!

Sometimes my big cousin looks after me.
We run races and have fun on the swings,
but if he wants to wrestle and play tickling
games, and I don't want to ...

No Means No!

We can build a giant sandcastle in the sand or play catch with a ball, but if I don't want to wrestle or play tickling games ...

No Means No!

When someone asks to hold my hand at school and I want to walk all by myself ...

No Means No!

Sometimes, I like to walk by myself and
I don't want to hold anyone's hand.

I can say, 'No thanks'
or 'Not today',
as kindly as I can.

When people ask me things and I say, 'No' …

I don't mean 'Maybe'
and I don't mean 'I'm not sure'.

What I REALLY mean is **No!**

So even though I may be small ...

I am strong and I have a voice that is
LOUD and **CLEAR**.

So ... when I say, 'No' ...

No Means No!

Discussion Questions for Parents, Caregivers and Educators

The following Discussion Questions are intended as a guide and can be used to initiate an open and honest dialogue with your child. Allow your child time to answer the questions and to ask some of their own. As your child grows and in daily conversations, ask them how they are feeling about a situation, what choices they wish to make and if they are okay with various activities. It is important that you value their input and listen to their voice. 'No Means No!' can be used as a teaching springboard for discussions on respect, rights, consent, personal boundaries and choice. All of these discussions only increase your child's sense of self, their confidence and empowerment.

Pages 4–5

Ask: Has anyone tried to kiss or hug you like this? How did you feel about it? What did you do? What can you do if you don't want to kiss or hug someone? *That's right! You could give them a polite and friendly high five, shake the person's hand or blow them a kiss if you know them quite well.*

Pages 6–7

Ask: Do you always have to kiss or hug a person, especially an adult? Why? Why not? (Note: It is a good idea to ask your child how they would like to greet or say goodbye to someone. By asking them and allowing them to choose, it shows that you respect their choice.) **Ask:** Do you think the little girl's parents are cross at how she is greeting Auntie Jeanie? Why not? *That's right! They understand she has the right to say, 'No!' and greet Auntie Jeanie in a way she is comfortable with. We all have an invisible personal 'bubble' around us and people need to ask permission to enter this personal space. We can choose to let them in or not.*

Pages 8–11

Ask: Where are your private parts? *Yes! They are your private body parts under your swimsuit.* (Note: Children should know the correct anatomical names for their private parts. The mouth is also a private part.) **Ask:** Do you think you are old enough to wash and dry your private parts? Why do you say that? **Say:** Remember, you are the boss of your body and if anyone touches your private parts, you can say, 'Stop!' loudly and then quickly go and tell one of the five people on your Safety Network.

(Note: Please see 'Some Secrets Should Never Be Kept' and/or 'Body Safety Education — A parents' guide to protecting kids from sexual abuse' for in-depth and comprehensive information on safe and unsafe touch, also known as Body Safety or child sexual abuse prevention education; please go to e2epublishing.info for details).

Pages 12–15

Ask: Do you have an older brother/sister/cousin you play with? Do they listen to you when you say, 'No' to a game? What could you do if they don't listen and respect your 'No'? *Yes! You could tell a trusted adult.* **Ask:** Do you always have to do what an older person says — especially if they ask you to play a game you don't want to? *That's right! Just because the person is older doesn't mean you have to play the game.* **Say:** The older cousin in the story respected the little girl's choice and didn't play the tickling game. They both played another game instead. Remember you are the boss of your body and if you don't want to play a certain game, such as tickling or wrestling, you don't have to.

(Note: Some sexual predators will use physical games, such as tickling, wrestling and encouraging a child to ride on their back to groom the child and have them become comfortable with the physical touch. Overtime, this touch may become sexual in nature. Of course, we want our children to enjoy games that involve physical contact but the child must always be a happy and willing participant. As soon as they become uncomfortable or don't want to play that game anymore, their 'No' should be adhered to and respected, and the game should cease immediately.)

Pages 16–19

Ask: If someone wants to hold your hand or give you a hug and you don't want them to, what can you do? *That's right! You can say, 'No!' or 'I don't like that' or 'Stop!'*
Say: Remember, you have your own invisible 'bubble' around you and if anyone comes inside your bubble, you have the right to say, 'No! I don't like that.'
 Ask: Imagine you wanted to hold someone's hand, and when you asked them they said, 'No!' What could you say and do? What if your teacher or another adult asks you to hold their hand or another child's hand when you are crossing a road — should you hold hands for your own safety? **Say:** Look at the boy. Is he worried or angry that the little girl did not want to hold is hand? *That's right! He is not worried or angry at all because he knows the little girl can make her own choices and he respects her choice not to hold his hand.* **Ask:** Why did the little girl say, 'No' in a kind way? *Yes! She did not want to hurt the boy's feelings but she still wanted to make her own choice and not hold his hand.*

Pages 20–21

Ask: What does this picture tell us about the little girl? *That's right! She is strong and important; and she is the boss of her body.* **Ask:** Can you stand like this little girl? How does it make you feel?

Pages 22–23

Say: Remember, you are the boss of your body and you have the right to say, 'No!' to any kind of touch that makes you feel uncomfortable. **Ask:** What should you do if someone touches you in a way that makes you feel unsafe? *That's right! You must get away quickly and Tell! Tell! Tell! You must keep on telling until you are believed.* **Ask:** What could you do if you saw someone else bully or not respect another person's 'No!'? *That's right! You can tell them that they have the right to say, 'No!' in a loud and clear voice. You can also tell a trusted adult.* **Ask:** Do you have any questions you would like to ask me?

About the Author

Jayneen Sanders (aka Jay Dale) is an experienced early years educator, author, publisher and blogger.

Jayneen writes children's books on Body Safety, consent, gender equality, respectful relationships and emotional intelligence. She believes empowering children from an early age makes for empowered teenagers and adults. Her titles include: *Some Secrets Should Never Be Kept*; *No Means No!*; *My Body! What I Say Goes!*; *No Difference Between Us*; *Pearl Fairweather, Pirate Captain*; *You, Me and Empathy* and her parents' guide *Body Safety Education*.

Jayneen is Lead Author for the children's literacy series *Engage Literacy* published by Capstone Classroom, and has written over 100 titles in that series. Jayneen is importantly a mother of three daughters and has always advocated for their empowerment.

Jayneen's ongoing passion for the safety and empowerment of children continues today with new manuscripts and free-to-download Body Safety resources always in the wings.

Her work can be found at **www.e2epublishing.info**

Books by the Same Author

My Body! What I Say Goes!

A children's picture book to empower and teach children about personal Body Safety, feelings, safe and unsafe touch, private parts, secrets and surprises, consent and respect. This book provides everything a child needs to know to help keep them safe from inappropriate touch. Discussion Questions included. Ages 3 to 9 years.

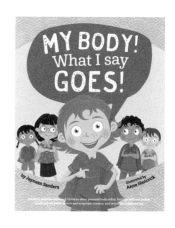

Some Secrets Should Never Be Kept

This beautifully illustrated children's picture book sensitively broaches the subject of safe and unsafe touch. This book will assist parents, caregivers and educators to broach this subject with children in a non-threatening and age-appropriate way. Discussion Questions included. Ages 3 to 11 years.

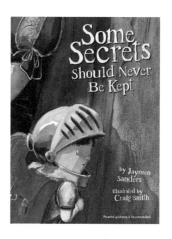

You, Me and Empathy

This charming story uses verse, beautiful illustrations and a little person called Quinn to model the meaning of empathy. Quinn shows an abundance of understanding, compassion and kindness towards others. Empathy is a learnt trait, and one to nurture in all children. Included are Discussion Questions and activities to promote empathy. Ages 3 to 9 years.

No Difference Between Us

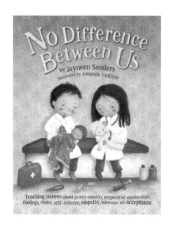

This beautifully illustrated children's book raises awareness around gender equality, respectful relationship, feelings, choice, self-esteem, tolerance and acceptance. In order to reduce gender-based violence, we need to teach children gender equality and respectful relationships from the earliest of years. Discussion Questions included. Ages 2 to 9 years.

Pearl Fairweather, Pirate Captain

Captain Pearl Fairweather is a brave, fair and strong pirate captain. She and her diverse crew of twenty-four women sail the seven seas on the good ship, *Harmony*, looking only for adventure. This beautifully illustrated book sets out to empower young girls to be strong, assertive and self-confident and for boys to respect, value and embrace that empowerment. Discussion Questions included. Ages 5 to 12 years.

Body Safety Education

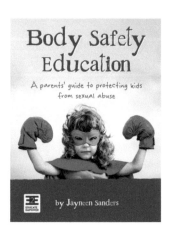

An essential step-by-step guide for parents, caregivers and educators on how to protect children from sexual abuse. This guide contains simple, practical and age-appropriate ideas and activities, as well as important information for adults on grooming, signs of abuse and disclosure responses.